The Red Light Was My Mind

The Red Light Was My Mind

Gary Charles Wilkens

Texas Review Press
Huntsville, Texas

FIRST EDITION, 2007
Requests for permission to reproduce material from this work should be sent to:

   Permissions
   Texas Review Press
   English Department
   Sam Houston State University
   Huntsville, TX 77341-2146

Cover painting by Amanda Willson
Cover design by Paul Ruffin

Acknowledgments:
"Boy's Haircut Seen at a Street Party" initially appeared in *The Texas Review*.

Library of Congress Cataloging-in-Publication Data

Wilkens, Gary Charles.
   The red light was my mind / Gary Charles Wilkens. -- 1st ed.
      p. cm.
   ISBN-13: 978-1-933896-04-5 (pbk. : alk. paper)
   ISBN-10: 1-933896-04-3 (pbk. : alk. paper)
   I. Title.
   PS3623.I5454R43 2007
   811'.6--dc22
                                       2007012422

These poems are for my beloved wife Anja, without whom they would not exist and I would not exist.

Table of Contents

The Red Light Was My Mind

The Devil Prefers the Blues

Lucifer addresses Michael:

Just don't rumple the suit, that's all I ask.
It used to belong to Johnson himself—
you didn't think I'd settle for his soul?

But long as you and the rest of the feather-brains
are comin' down to do the Old Man's dirty work
again, there's a few things you should know:

I never tempted a man who didn't ask for it,
I never spoiled any heart not black already,
I never took any virgins who didn't call me.

You'd like to believe, all you puffed-up birds,
that *I* ruined God's pampered darlings,
that it takes a Satan to make a sinner.

The truth is God's little dust babies are defective,
broke, all a shambles—men need no help to slaughter,
need no coaxing to cheat, need no leading to lie—

I could tell you more, including some interesting
stories about Eve and a certain snake, but I've
urgent appointments elsewhere.

The Hard Objects of the World

C.J. Burdett had swallowed a library globe,
that belly of his bursting a checkered shirt
in the north Mississippi sun.
His cigar twitched.
The blacks and migrants in the fields
he surveyed knew him as a master
of the hard objects of the world—
the dirt-caked steel of the harvester,
the sharp rocks and the rifle muzzle.
He knew himself as a master
of the hard object that spun the globe.

Angela's Locket

I.   Done Got Old

Burdett's Ford sloshes through mud
and the veil of flies that rules the road,
olive light peeling like fading paint.

The headlights grab rutted driveway
and yank him up to the rotted shack,
probing it like a doctor's cold fingers.

The workers' hovel looks blank and bent.
Burdett spits his snuff and shouts
for his migrant men to come outside.

Like ants after a flood two lean blacks
appear in the yard and shuffle to the truck,
slumping down inside its leaf-strewn bed.

Burdett throws his machine along the road
into the darkening willow swamp
until it slams to a stop by a fat oak.

The three men peer by flashlight
into the soup of night and mosquitoes.
Burdett barks them into digging the murk.

After long they hear a sharp clack
and Burdett curses. Dark hands haul
the iron chest from slimy muck.

Burdett shoves the men to the side,
rips off the lock and thrusts a claw
into the jumble of rusted junk.

The old locket in his rough grip
is purple with a back of gold—
he shakes it toward the sunken men.

He cranks up the truck almost before
the mud-numbed men pile into the back
and drops them beside the broken house.

The locket lies open next to him,
a woman's gray stare freezing upon
his sweating and tearing cheeks.

II.   Please Don't Leave Me Right Now

Angela trembled into the jade porch chair,
alone before the empty house of evening,
a glass of watery tea beading beside her.

Crickets screamed like souls stuck in hell,
gnarled fingers of trees shrouding
fields full of faceless laboring men.

She felt weak as the creaking wind,
fumbling for the green cup of pills
the doctor had left with a quiet word.

They didn't help, and heat pulled pain
from hollowing bones that cheated her
out of day and barred her from night.

Charles was out there, she knew, driving
negroes like man-shaped machines,
uneasy until the cotton was in its bin.

She coughed and shuddered. She hadn't
touched his warm chest in weeks,
she had not been held while she vomited.

Her work lay beside the tea glass, a purple
locket of the type her mother had taught
her to make, had given to Angela's father.

It was complete save for the picture.
She held it close to her eyes and blinked.
A cold vessel for a cold message.

Dark had dropped full on her by now,
hiding her thoughts from herself. That was
good, she thought, slipping in the photo.

A man stood beside her rows of geraniums.
His skin was the hue of the shielding night.
He came and took the locket, took her lips.

He would place the locket some place damp,
some place suiting its dim love, some place
from which it could deliver its black whisper.

Burdett's Monologue

Burdett you ugly racist!
Burdett you fat swine—
men called you this who've never
seen a sow laid up with eight runts
sucking her sack!

A man who grabs a gun when he's threatened!
Who works a field and gets the cotton in.
Who's seen blood turn soil to dirt.
Who's seen men become piles of flies!

Burdett, you slick pile of guts,
you know how to keep high rollers true,
you know how hard objects push
in slow low places, how shit
fills up the tub!

Burdett, she wasn't true.
Truth is what a man like you needs.
Truth is what a man like you earns.
Burdett she was a harvested field.
Fields that don't yield get burned.

Burdett, you old sick shoe!
What's become of you?
Have you taken to lighting candles?
Taken to sitting up blank nights?
Piss and shit!

Burdett, you old soldier.
Keep marching man.
You'll see cotton gathered yet.

Leaving Burdett's Plantation

Yellow mud runs in the river,
blood burns on his knife.
The beat guitar in wire hands
strums a sun-boiled song
in haze of slow Delta dawn.
He leaves behind him rotted windows
fallen into high-grown grass.
The bluesman walks his way
along the dull asphalt snake of I 40.

Three Hours Down a Dirt Road

In green North Mississippi heat,
slappin' flies from greasy necks,
we pulled up to a shack
with a burp of gravel
near a town called Senatobia
and found one hell of a harp player
passed out on the front porch.

Crammed inside the one-room house
were twenty booze-drenched men
stinking on a Sunday afternoon
and shooting craps. They hooted at us
and shoved evil-smelling whiskey
into our hands. Fred sat down
with his guitar and bottleneck—
walls were soon burnin',
men wavin' like willows.

A little later Johnny dragged himself in,
a thick fog in his eyes.
He rummaged through his pockets
for his harp as Fred launched into
"Shake 'Em on Down"—a shrill bird sang
to the whang of the guitar, cuttin'
a sound like a spurned lady's cry.

Later that Night

Colored beads rattle on coffee skin,
breasts sway and honey drips,
bluesmen bend strings in rosy light—
rhythm spills and melody trips
as ladies smile and birds take flight.

Blind Jefferson

I was born blind, though when I was a boy
I could see light in one eye. Blindness never
troubled me much—it was mine and I owned it.
Other men were blinder than myself.

Soon as I was big enough I took up the six-string
and never put the old thing down. I picked with my
    fingers
the song of muddy angels singing in a swamp.
I picked along midnight roads, dark carnivals and
    sweet joints.

I was born in corn-rows, raised in a dirt and river
    shack,
rising every morning to the motherless breeze
    moanin'.
It gurgled a deep water creek that flowed with weeds,
wrinkled leaves and long grass from the field.

Clarksdale, 1933

Green paint banging off the rotted screen door,
Floyd steps silently onto the dirty porch.
Herman rests there in the low wood chair,
battered banjo braced between the brown stained
knees of his worn work pants. Floyd hears Momma
humming "Just a Little Talk with Jesus" in the
    kitchen.
A dog barks a biting flat note as the shot kicks
Herman back against the wall, breaking a pot of
    petunias.

White Trash

When I was a boy Momma sent me to the store
with a five dollar bill to get a bottle of Clorox,
only she didn't mean the brand name but any old
bleach that would serve to scrub stains and make
our worn clothes white as our poor skin.

No Drink, No Fries

After splurging on a science fiction novel I had barely
enough for a plain hamburger, no drink, no fries,
at the Mr. Burger. Mom wouldn't like what I had
    done
with the change from the jug of milk but wouldn't
hit me for it. As long I got home before it got warm.
She understood some things. I had to insist to the
    guy
behind the counter I wanted no drink, no fries.

Boy's Haircut Seen at a Street Party

When I was a kid we called that a *rattail*.
With a rattail, odds were you lived in a trailer park.
Your momma made you bologna sandwiches
and you liked 'em. You ate government cheese. You
ran down the street with gnats and heat at twilight.
Your folks had never married and your momma had a
boyfriend or three. Your bike was older than you
    were.
You loved too much sugar in the red berry Kool-Aid.
Odds were you'd grow up to have a kid with a rattail.

Blue House

Suddenly I remembered the smell and taste of grapes
    that grew
on Grandmother's small vinery next to the blue house
    built
when she was a young mother. Hiding behind lush
    vines I feasted
on purple globes until face and fingers were stained
    and toes
sunk in damp sand. Fat pillars holding up the dark
    vines were
riddled with rot. Silence lingered long within walls of
    grape
even when rain thundered.

Sworn Testimony, Johnson R., Yazoo County Mississippi

Hell. I don't give a damn.
Me sellin' my soul to the Devil's true,
and it wudn't no stupid thing neither.
Rekkin I know a few things the Devil don't.
Spose ever good man's got a better Angel
lookin' out fer'm. Ain't my time to go
anyhow. I'm a bad man myself jus' plain
as day, and the Devil can't put hooves
on a soul that's already burnin'.

I was playin' these little dances for years
to keep off the farm, never makin' no money.
That damn Patton act like he possessed anyhow.
I jus' done him one better. He ain't got nuttin'
now. I got womens crawlin' all over my kingsnake!
I got up one morning from a lady's bed and snuck out.
She wasn't nuttin' but a no-good doney.

I was like to go back home, got ramblin' on my mind
most days. Ran down to the station and caught
the first mail train I seen. Ain't had nuttin' but
my suit and guitar. I would set in the car and play
the blues all day when the train run by the river,
runnin' deep green like a cut vein. I cry ever time
I think about it.

So I get off in some little town what ain't but
a store and a church I rekkin. You know they don't
want no playin' in there. Couldna find no place
to lay my head or no food. Then I see this old
        momma,
she makin' eyes at me sayin' *you better come on*

in my kitchen cause it goin' to be rainin' out there.
I was never a man to turn down a little jellyroll.
We spent a nice little time together, she all over me.
Come night she wantin' to put me out. I ast her why
and she begin to moan sayin' *daddy you got to go.*
Some man come in and he shoutin'. I grab my pants
and run out. Who is it? Damn Patton!

I ran outta there and got way outta town, sure as hell.
Po' Bob done come on a cold night to crossroads, the
    moon
was like a bone. I's wonderin' what evil have I done.
I was jus' there playin' my guitar til some nice feller
come up dressed like a million dollars. He one slick
    pretty
piece, some city dude I rekkin.

He done asked what I's doin' and I told'm. He up and
    say
he the Devil, jus' like that. Course I don't bleeve'm.
He ast if he could tune my guitar. I told'm to go to
    hell.
He say he jus' come from there. I let'm take it and play
a few notes. Sound like a thousand souls screamin' in
    fire,
it did.

He give it back and ast if I want to play like that.
I say hell yeah mister. So he make me sign. I can't
    make
but a X but he say it's enough. My guitar sing like a
    demon.
I fell down on my knees to thank'm but he jus' laugh.
All of a sudden he gone. I felt cold and lonesome
    right then
but sure can play. All that matters, I rekkin.

Then couldna Patton or House or any of them slick
    dudes
play like me! It's damn sure. They on the way out.
It's gonna be me King one day. I ain't worried 'bout
    no Devil
takin' my soul—ain't ever good man got a better
    Angel
lookin' out fer'm? Hell. I don't give a damn.

Shot a Man Dead Blues

House had the judge's word ringing in his ears—
"Never set foot in this town again, boy,
never bring back them Devil Blues!"

Gray rain drilled holes beside the tracks
and put a lump in the bottom of his heart,
the last spark of Clarksdale fading behind

bent trees. House trembled and shook off
cold fingers peeling out his soul.
His little bag slipped off a soaked shoulder.

"You done shot a man dead, boy, done took
human life and you's fit to die, to die
and never see the land of grace."

House thought he might make it to Lula,
to some lady with a bottle of corn whisky,
to some hot nasty joint and get hisself

killed in a fight, or play the blues 'til
they ran him off again. The dirty Blues
had killed a preacher's soul, took it straight

to stinkin' sulphur Hell—he had done got old
in a single night, done buried hope of love.
House spat out the bitter taste of blue-gray.

Lula, MS

His eyes disappeared into the back of his head.
The joint was saucy and sweet with orange glows
and lily dresses bulging with big shuffling legs—

Patton sat back in the crowd with a woman on each
    arm
and whiskey whistling through his teeth,
cheering and jeering as House dug his grave on stage.

House strummed one chord like swinging an axe.
He was cutting the cord that held him in this room
crimson with its river of stained souls crying mad.

He sought to curry no favor. He dug the bones of
    grief.
If Blues could kill a man, he asked it to take
and nail him to the cross of this world.

Juke Joint

You don't want a woman who
argue, fuss and fight,
Patton sang, stomping the stage
with his big black shoe.

You just want a woman to
barrelhouse all the night,
Patton growled, pounding the box
with his hard right hand.

Everybody did every dance they knew
and the walls shook with fright.
Billy laid his hat down
and took after some big momma.

Stag O'Lee never drank too few
and kept his face out of the light,
searching around for his Stetson
with its fake leather band.

Patton churned the crowd
Into a tumble with all his might—
Stag stumbled out
Wearing Billy's too-small hat.

Stag O'Lee

I.

Stag O'Lee was a bad man.
Rain feared to wet him,
sunlight feared to warm him.
Stag slept with .44 in hand.

Stag stood beside a house
where a porch light burned
a hole in the sack of night.
Stag cursed the man inside.

Stag banged on the widow
and hollered for his hat.
"You done stole my Stetson
and now you got to die!"

Billy rubbed his eyes and hushed
his wife back to sleep.
"What? Will you kill a man
'bout a five dollar Stetson hat?"

"Can't you see I got a darling wife
and two little lovin' babes?"
Have your ol' hat back and get
on down the road!"

"What I care 'bout your darling wife
and two little lovin' babes!"
"You done stole my Stetson hat
now I'm bound to take your life!"

Stag drew his pistol and waved it
through the window. He fired once

and missed and he fired twice
and missed but the third took Billy's life.

Stag O'Lee was a bad man
and he ran from the scene of the crime,
five dollar Stetson still lying there
in the dust with its fake leather band.

II.

Tom Rushen was the High Sheriff
of the county and didn't take
to no juke jointing, no moonshining,
no ramblin' in his domain.

He was a broad man two sizes too big
and carried two pistols the size of the law—
he aimed to arrest Patton and drive whiskey
out of the minds of men who would be good.

Rushen was on the trail of some bad rambler
when they ran up to him crying "Oh Sheriff,
Oh Sheriff, you gotta come on now—Stag O'Lee
done shot po' Billy for a five dollar Stetson hat!"

"I'm ta chase him down and bring him in,
sure as mercy I am." said Rushen, and he ran
after that bad black man as fast as rabbit can
and found him laying easy down by the creek.

"Listen here, Stag O'Lee, you got to come with me,
'cause you done killed po' Billy and you's bound for
        jail."
Rushen had Stag in the sights of his two guns
and would not let him run.

Stag jumped up with his .44 in hand but the law
shot first and brought him down. Stag lay on the
   ground
pleading for his life, begging mercy from the Lord.
"You can't see what you ain't never shown," Rushen
   said.

Stag O' Lee came before the Judge who swung
the fat gavel down— "You kill a man for a five dollar
   Stetson hat—
don't no one need you anymore in this life! We gonna
send you to the only place you to deserve to rest!"

On a morning dark they drove Stag O'Lee out
to the Gallis Pole and by hand of man he hung,
swinging by the neck like a gourd in the wind,
and they's all glad to see him die.

Chant of Peetie Wheatstraw

Wheatstraw was the evilest lick
the guitarist knew—
he was blood on the string,
he was the Devil's son-in-law,
he was the High Sheriff of Hell,
he was rollin' and tumblin',
he was barrelhouse,
he was jellyroll,
he was burnin' lights
on the killin' floor,
he was the evil woman
with love on her mind,
he was the evilest lick
the guitarist knew.

Charley Patton's Grave

Charley Patton's grave
new and shiny gray,
Charley Patton's grave
grabbed by yellow grass—
Charley Patton's grave
with broken whisky bottle.

Howl for Holiday

Billie played with beat and melody,
danced with sex and sin, drugs and booze,
sang with the howl of the horn,
toyed with men dark as midnight rivers,
heat like summer fire on their breath,
their hands coiled snakes on her breasts.

In little clubs tucked into corners
of wasted streets she had her own
when she dropped behind a beat,
when she cried her blues down—
she sang as a horn.

Men Don't Know What the Little Girl Understands

Momma only makes chicken and pork-n-beans
on Saturday nights when Poppa is off at
a joint playing guitar with whiskey-breath men.

I can smell meat popping in grease
and the oniony tang of simmering beans
as she works by bare kitchen bulb

after sending me to bed, creaky phonograph
spitting nasty dance blues. She giggles
and whistles like a happy bird in a beech.

I'm drifting to sleep when I hear the back door
screech open and slam closed. Momma squeals
like she never done for Poppa no way.

Vicksburg Woman

Her eyes spoke sad and gentle blues
to gray woods and wilted weeds
as she rocked on her shack's porch,
feeling rambling wind toss
her black hair in the tan evening,
watching the hobo sun go down.

Follow Me Boy

The drive through the dusk from Vicksburg had been
     hard
and the hoodoo woman's hut was sunk into a swamp.
Penny clutched her bag and stepped over weedy mud
to pound the little door hanging like a man on the
     gallows.

A crow's voice called her in. The hoodoo woman was
     a mass
of ancient blankets from which stuck two withered
     talons.
A straw hat perched atop a pile of grape vine locks—
two fireballs peered out from a heavy-breathing body.

Penny could make out little of the tools and traps
     that sat
about the old woman, if she was even old or a
     woman—
it could have been a demon, it could have been the
     Devil
muttering low *what is your wish this cold night?*

Penny stuttered she wanted some spell, some potion,
to make a certain man do her bidding, to win the love
of a man who would not quit rambling and settle
     down
to a warm home and a good woman, a full dinner
     plate.

The woman exploded with screeching and whooping.
She shook and rocked like willow fronds and snorted.
You want de love or you want de man's ol' root?
she laughed, reaching for a bunch of bags on her
     table.

Penny looked down and mumbled a little prayer.
Just a love potion, just some stuff to make a man be
    true.
*Ain't no such thing, girl! De mens all be ramblers and do
no woman no good!* But she thrust a crimson sachet at
    Penny.

*Drip the oil on your bosom, bathe in crystal salts, burn
    incense,
use Follow Me Boy and dat man will follow you!
It have de catnip, damiana, and calamus root, it have
    woman
magic dat keep de mens close to de 'ol honey pot!*

Penny gingerly dropped the bag into her hers and left
    silver
in the woman's gnarled palm, gushing thanks and
    backing out
out into wailing wind that bit into her coats, feeling a
    glow
in her legs and deep rhythm in her breath.

I put a spell on you

You're mine because oak leaves hang heavy
in twilight air blue with scent of sex,
because whisky winks in the glass when my hair
falls over your face as you lean in to tease
my lips with yours, because the sheen of sweat
lingers on your skin. The last sight I see tonight
is the hoodoo root that hangs above our bed.

Hot Tamales and They're Red Hot

He reminded Penny of the Blues song
about the black man in the black Cadillac
with white teeth and white eyes,
a black boy with a shiny toy—

but he was a gentleman who brought a lollipop
for little Henry each time he came to take Penny
out to coffeehouses or dances, where once
they shook and moaned to Johnson—

she felt the Devil in his hands as they lay
at the small of her back on the strings of her dress—
rhythm pounding their bodies, fear forgotten,
fires dancing, her devil grinding in her hips.

Jack Johnson was a Boxer (July 4, 1910)

Jack Johnson was a big man,
Jack Johnson was a black man,
Jack Johnson was a sad man,
Jack Johnson was hated for his skin.

Jack Johnson drove fast cars,
Jack Johnson lived in high circles,
Jack Johnson danced in bright halls,
Jack Johnson loved white women.

Jack Johnson won against white men,
Jack Johnson shamed white society,
Jack Johnson wounded white pride,
Jack Johnson faced the Great White Hope.

Jack Johnson started slow,
Jack Johnson landed hard,
Jack Johnson moved quick,
Jack Johnson sent his man down.

Jack Johnson was vilified,
Jack Johnson was hunted,
Jack Johnson was driven out,
Jack Johnson was just the man he was.

Jack Johnson was a big man,
Jack Johnson was a black man,
Jack Johnson was a sad man,
Jack Johnson was hated for his skin.

Seven Line Odes

1. John Lee Hooker

Well my momma didn't allow me
just to stay out all night long . . .
I didn't care what momma didn't allow . . .
I said YES people . . .
Boogie Chillen . . .
and I felt so good . . .
that I boogied just the same . . .

2. Rev. Gary Davis

One morning I was walking along
I heard the angels singing . . .
reckon what they said to me?
Sins have been forgiven
and my soul's set free . . .
I was down on my knee,
I heard the angels singing . . .

3. Robert Johnson

Followed her to the station
with a suitcase in my hand,
and I looked her in the eye . . .
All my love's in vain,
All my love's in vain,
the blue light was my blues,
the red light was my mind . . .

Bluesman in Europe

i. About seven of ten European women
could be politely called "thin."
Nothing some good Southern cooking
couldn't fix, though. Get these ladies
some fried chicken, mashed potatoes,
collard greens, corn bread and
sweet peach iced tea and they'd be
fit to take to juke joint or back room.

ii. They sell beer everywhere here,
even on Sundays! And they'll have it
with breakfast, lunch, and dinner, too.
But that's just the start—there are
more types of wine, whiskey, and
every hard drink here than at
a Tennessee mountain wedding.
Strong stuff, too, and they drink it
like water—once I saw a man drink
wine seven hours straight then walk
home three miles on a cold night.
Folks back home could take lessons . . .

iii. What they call a small church here
could count as a cathedral back home.
I swear I don't know how the church
ladies raised the money—must have had
some fierce bake sales. Them churches're
real old and fancy, though, so I reckon
they had some time. The pastor stands
up in a little box and says a bunch
a funny words into deep gray walls.
The idea is to get over the power of God.
Sometimes if ya go in all alone
you can almost feel it.

Travelin' Riverside Hobo Blues

You're not bound by schedules, bills, job expectations,
    or the IRS,
but by hard dirt on the tracks, cold stars of the open
    night.

You live where you want, sleep where you want, go
    where you want—
if the long iron snakes will pour through the dark firs
    goin' that way.

You never pay fare unless you want to—never rent,
    gas, nor water,
never taxes unless except for lonesome fires in
    darkened rail yards.

You share a rich man's freedom and a poor man's
    tears, a poison
tender, sweet, seductive—just to see ramblin' rivers
    slip by.

Your old lady calls herself Freedom—her soft arms are
    your pillow.
Her hair's dusky scent leads you to jump trains every
    rainy day.

You hear a train whistle, you see a moving train, train
    cars, train tracks—
once again you're travelin' 'til you catch that old
    Westbound.

Spring Poem Aborted

The sky was a child's unenthusiastic use
of the "Light Gray" crayon, depicting a day
too cool to run in pungent grass, trapping
all shades of green in the box, while blues
and silvers and browns spilled onto paper
like the notes of a concert no one came to.

Natural Blues

Rain wept with the telling
of the sky's sorrows,
Spring's blush of green hung
with the dripping day's wait
as Nature blubbed into its coffee cup,
singin' *we're so sad, so sad,*
low-down lonely and sad—
the sweet-corn sun she has gone
and left us to shiver and moan.

By the Dark Woods Cabin

The chipped and faded concrete Mary
stood in a dry fountain by a red shack
in the woods, covered with dirt
and abandoned wispy spider webs,
hands together and head
slanted down, silent and waiting.

Sorrow, part I

This morning was the thickest since I started.
Dawn made an effort to appear, but once light
broke light shower changed to heavy rain.
Each day seems a ghost of real experience.

Sky flat gray, fog in the upper reaches of the hills.
The rain is poured from a bottle.
The bottle is lonely and the bottle is me.
The bottle is a guard keeping watch night and day.

A few minutes of truant night, a gentle breeze,
then light comes up behind me, a magic moment
    lost.
I can see it, feel it, but can't get it on paper.
A five minute experience under heavy gray downpour.

Sorrow, part II

The air that morning was a gray sheet on an unmade
　　bed—
itself a sign she was gone, for she never left an untidy
　　bed,
except when she left it for good.

The trees along the road to the office were a gallery
of snarling hecklers, who found it very rich indeed
　　that love
had turned out to be a released fish that sank, dead
　　anyway.

Blues Nazm

I could only love her when she pushed me down—
anger faded to sadness as the sun went down.

The river reeds dipped heavy into silver pools—
I sent my tears away with a heart bent down.

Gray clouds masked pale trembling stars—
I couldn't hear the name the rain sent down.

The cloud of birds scattered from dark water—
I was lonely as the last leaf the trees lent down.

Nothing was ever so quiet as when her laugh faded—
the hanging violets never let any scent down.

Mississippi Highway

Slate clouds march in thick
troops over cut wheat,

the shade of the road falls
bit by bit to dark blue,

raindrop pointilism
upon the window pane.

Wind-lashed rain streams sideways
under a struggling umbrella,

her hair braided in brown strands
across her cheeks,

red petals shivers in cautious light
as clouds curl away.

Bury Me By the Highway Side

Turtle bones lie in wild grass—
a cracked shell, half missing.

The wrinkled olive skin is alive
with black ants carrying out

the work given to the world
of little things when giants fall.

Dirty limbs wait for years to pass
and the sinking that brings release

to tired forms that gave up yesterday—
past lives and old pains become wheat.

A New Creation

The engine sun was reincarnation. He'd been taken
from his cell early,
fed something decidedly better than usual prison fare,
dressed in new clothes,
spent the morning in offices and waiting rooms while
paper work was filed
and final confirming calls made, wondering if this
was some version
of what souls in limbo went through waiting to be
reborn.

Two silent guards came, who could have been angels
for all he knew.
They led him slowly through doors and gates, sounds
and smells increasing
as the spiritual world dropped level by level into the
material world—
at every door more sandpaper sunlight.

They walked down a short hall to a set of heavy iron
gates which creaked back
and spilled in the outside world: a stinging river of
trees and birds and dirt roads
beyond the prison walls. He walked out alone, his
companions falling back
and sealing the doors shut. He stood on gray gravel
with his small suitcase,
forehead misting from August heat.

Soul Food

The little evangelical church where the Holy Spirit
found rhythm had crouched in the neighborhood
where elderly black ladies wore red head wraps.
With wide hips and bellies in flower-print dresses
they keep their drives clean with long handled
    brushes.
They potted red-orange marigolds in late afternoon.
Now it's a soul food shop, a slanted house
with no windows. The screen door is always open
and gnats buzz your eyes in watery sunlight—
it still has a black cross on the tan roof.

Leroy's House of Catfish

Leroy would have stood in the shower longer,
letting hot streams bake him into a pinkish white
    man
or a piece of salmon, but the store had to be opened.

The house had jade tile floors and gold window
    frames,
the stink of frying fish and coleslaw its atmosphere.
Hushpuppies sat obediently and begged.

Leroy gave Bertha her daily cigarette and let her stand
out where she could watch pickup trucks fly by the
    sign
of Fred the fat crab who announced the $5.95 buffet.

Leroy's World Famous Mississippi Catfish

Trina was a seventeen year old who waited tables.
She spent Leroy's money on crystal meth.
Her bouncy strawberry rings made men
give big tips and drop lewd hints.
Leroy once tried to get her clean,
get her to live with him.
It ended badly on a blood orange Sunday morning.

Leroy's Women

Leroy was a black man with a small potbelly
and a thin mustache. The palms of his wide hands
were nearly white. After the last French had fried
on Friday nights Leroy liked to use those hands
to entertain white women beneath blinking lights
in his shag living room to sounds of Bobby Bland.

Bertha's Kitchen

Call her Big Black Bertha and she'll knock your white
    ass out.
Make sweet to her by complimenting her strawberry
    pie—
all north Mississippi knows of Heaven.
Her hair net strains to hold in the shiny hump on her
    head.
Beneath a metal table in her tidy and efficient kitchen
she sips from a black bottle she calls her Assistant.

Leroy Gets the Holy Ghost

The Reverend Fidley T. Doakes preaches weekly
to the God-fearing folks, although he knows some
have their minds on tartar sauce and lemon rinds.
One Sunday after Service he came to lunch
and made Leroy nervous. With Bible in one hand,
fork of catfish in the other, he lectured his Brother
on how Christ had split fish by faith. Leroy said
Amen and took the Lord's name his own way.

Hard Work Blues

Joe knows how to work a dozer,
how metal tracks respond to braking.
He is one with a dozer, hell with a dozer,
sitting atop one in gumbo and gravel,
driving deeper into the Devil's dirt.

Joe knows how low to drop
the blade when the ground isn't dry,
how much earth can be pushed
and how far, if the juice stick
should be closer to the rabbit
than to the turtle. Joe also knows
answers to a heap more
questions along these lines.

Blues Walking like a Man (Joe brings his work home)

A walk of tears and rain, too old too young,
of dark night and daybreak, raw like
Mississippi morning sun, walking
dirt roads with dry throat and empty pockets.

Motion musical like the testament of wheat returning
to a burnt field, heavy like the heart of a man
　　working
alone to bury the love of his life who couldn't keep
her dresses down. A gunshot and a train headed
　　south.

Killing Floor

On a night black as Satan's shoe leather
a man with a shotgun marched under stars
sharp as the heart of a faithless lover.

Under the wide brim of his beaten hat
perched steel eyes and a set jaw—
trees shrank in shame as he passed.

From the battered shack came whiskey music,
lusty shouts from drunk men, tinkling laughter
from women in loose skirts scented with lilac.

The man paused by the broken door to listen.
A table crashed and the guitar screamed
like a strangled child. The man spat.

Anger split the doors like a tornado,
lights shimmered and fires sputtered,
walls collapsed in splintery pain.

When the killing was done the man stood
in the center of the floor crying, as a dog's
bark carried through the deep pine woods.

Levee Camp Holler

I cried "Redemption!"
when none was there,
I cried "Redemption!"
when all was bare.

I cried "Redemption!"
when none was there,
I cried "Redemption!"
when all was bare.

I cried "Redemption!"
when the Depression reigned,
I cried "Redemption!"
and the work leader came,
I cried "Redemption!"
and it was there.

I cried "Redemption!"
when none was there,
I cried "Redemption!"
when all was bare.

I cried "Redemption!"
when none was there,
I cried "Redemption!"
when all was bare.

I cried "Redemption!"
when waters were high,
I cried "Redemption!"
and the gold sun was nigh,
I cried "Redemption!"
and it was there.

I cried "Redemption!"
when none was there,
I cried "Redemption!"
when all was bare.

I cried "Redemption!"
when none was there,
I cried "Redemption!"
when all was bare.